To Archie & Rosie,
for the fun of read:

Major Payn
HAPPY BOTTOM
Peril and Promise

Written by Heather Chamberlain
Illustrated by Robin Edmonds

Heather Chamb

For my mum, Pearl

Chapter in Verse

Lost

The moon was high, the stars were bright
but in the barn in darkest night,
there came much rustling in the straw
with all minds on the day before.

Whilst Panic wept and no one slept,
thoughts of poor Monty were now kept
in broken hearts that would not mend
till they could search and find their friend.

"We must do somethin'," Scurry said.
"I don't believe that Monty's dead.
We need to plan what we could do
then find some way to see it through."

Winnie whinnied, Winston snorted,
sobbing Panic, though, retorted:
"Poor Monty's lost! I said don't go.
And where he is, we still don't know."

"True," said Olive. "And that is why
we'll draft in fowl to comb the sky.
At first light we'll check bay and beach,
then all the islands we can reach."

"I wanna fly, too," Scurry said.
"Been dreamin' of it in me 'ead.
Me eyes could 'elp to spy the land
as we sweep over sea an' sand."

"Well, if you do," said Olive owl,
"don't hitch a lift with hawk-like fowl.
Cos should you dare, I have a hunch
you might be treating them to lunch!"

The Switch

Major Payne, now at home from Spain,
and eager to open his door:
tripped on a lace, then fell without grace
to land in a heap on the floor.

Head took a bump, and he felt the lump.
Woofbot applied it with slobber.
And then, by gosh, he gave him a wash
so that he would not have to bother.

As he made tea, in came Marie
to hear all his holiday news.
He'd bought a phone, photos were shown,
most buttons, though, had him confused.

Marie, with news and press reviews
of jeep's daring dive in the Piddle,
told him the tale, and he took it well:
thought it a bit of a giggle.

Learning the truth, he hit the roof
(despite the fact jeep saved the Mayor).
It came to mind, that he must find
the culprit, for theft was not fair!

The next morning...

Roused from his sleep by a loud BEE-EE-EEP!
(which first he tried hard to ignore),
old sleepy-head rolled out of bed
when there came a knock on his door.

Traipsed off to see who it could be
(part-dressed in his slippers and shirt),
and to be sure, outside his door
found Wally, bright-eyed and alert.

Pip, who was Wally's old collie
was sniffing the plants in a tub.
The Major, bemused — was not amused
when it then cocked a leg on his shrub.

Wally'd towed JO3LL with his lorry
and parked him just outside the gate.
He'd gone from zero to hero
but was now left in fear of his fate.

Feeling stressed, the Major got dressed
and Wally strolled in for some tea.
Without a care, perched on a chair,
though none were less welcome than he.

Tea left to brew (Wally in the loo)
Major Payne hatched a dastardly deed:
punish Wally for his own folly —
a chicken shed he did not need.

Laxatives are the best thing by far
when you need, but can't go to, the loo.
Major Payne's tin had plenty left in,
so a dastardly plan was thought through.

The toilet flushed, so Major Payne rushed
to add laxative to a mug.
(A bad day or two, spent on the loo
would stop Wally looking so smug.)

Tea on a tray then came Wally's way
(plan, though, about to be scuppered).
Wally's mug switch met not a hitch,
when Major Payne went to his cupboard.

Sipping his brew, the Major soon knew
that he hadn't the mug he desired.
Wally did too, so said "Toodle-loo!"
The Major's "lax plan" had backfired!

Shimmy

The Major snored, sweet dream in head,
till tapping roused him from his bed.
It would be crows, he was quite sure:
they'd mocked him much like this before.

Rolled out of bed, kicked chamber pot
(he still remained a clumsy clot).
Then on one leg, in a pogo dance,
a trumpet sounded in his pants!

There rose a tune of several notes
as sound and pong in air did float.
Woofbot stuck a paw on his nose.
The Major cursed and rubbed his toes.

When crows then cawed, ignored the flock.
But drawing curtains — what a shock!
There on the roof, stood on the thatch,
humungous bird having a scratch.

He waved his arms, shooed bird away,
but peacock was in mood to stay.
So on his long neck, his head rose
to "kiss" the Major on the nose.

The Major fell back, bird hopped in
(a little scruffy, somewhat thin).
Poor thing was tired, he'd travelled far,
since he was kicked out of a car.

Downstairs, ear glued to mobile phone,
the Major chased it round his home.
His plan to scare it out the door
spread piles of poop across the floor!

The Major thought this most unfair,
more so, when it hijacked his chair.
He jumped and jigged, peacock bemused.
When he yelled, "GET OFF!", it refused.

No luck on the phone, seemed no-one cared,
though his concern was widely shared.
Learned many peacocks are disowned
and best to have poor thing re-homed.

Marie arrived, spied bird in chair
and, as she then approached with care,
"My word," she said, "I'd not have bet
you'd have a peacock as a pet!"

A brusque response soon let her know
the Major wanted it to go.
Marie responded, "Leave it be.
And I will get him out, you'll see."

And so she did. Food, as a bribe,
enticed the bird to go outside.
Then on the lawn, for now at least,
peacock enjoyed a welcome feast.

Marie watched peacock, quite in awe
(not been so close to one before).
He needed feeding, was so skinny,
and he thanked her with a shimmy.

Shimmy was full of grace and charm,
but in the barn caused much alarm:
Panic freaked out, as Scurry then shout:
"Don't want you 'ere. Go 'ome. Get out!"

Fireside, though, said, "Leave him alone.
We too came here seeking a home."
Once Shimmy had told them of his plight,
the mice agreed that she was right.

Shimmy was homed and now had friends.
But would this be his journey's end?
For now, at least, he could roost in hay
and be fed by Marie each day.

Sneak

A gull named Sneak, with a crooked beak,
now arrived, bringing hope to the barn:
Thought it was fair that he should now share
what he'd learned from the ospreys of Arne.

One sunny day, he flew there to say,
on an island quite far from their reach,
Monty'd been saved — washed up by the waves —
and was now just marooned on a beach.

Then in a flurry, Sneak took Scurry
high into the sky for a ride.
Said he must go, or they'd never know
whether Monty was dead or alive.

Their safe return had Scurry confirm
where Monty was — he was no more.
But he told his friends, it wasn't the end,
just because he was not on the shore.

He'd only know if they could now go
and conduct a big search on the ground.
Had a keen team for such a grand scheme,
if a seaworthy boat could be found.

Sadly, friends note, that without a good boat
they faced a heartbreaking decision.
Monty was mourned, for it had now dawned
that there would be no rescue mission.

Spooked

The hour was late, the moon was bright,
on what would prove a scary night.
In slumberland the Major snored,
but this night could not be ignored.

The eerie sense that filled the room
woke Major Payne, who through the gloom
had his heart filled with mortal dread:
when a spirit rose beside his bed.

The spirit told him, "Come with me.
There's something I wish you to see."
The Major was then whisked away
and feared he'd not see light of day.

Teeth a-chatter, skin like holly,
touching down by Rooster's Folly,
"You want things cheap," the spirit said:
"That's why you own a chicken shed!"

It then went on...

"Wally stood by me till the end.
And, far from bad, was my best friend.
You think he's dim, but that's not true:
he's made a monkey out of you!"

Whoosh! Up they went into the night,
poor Major Payne a sorry sight.
With spirit gone, fell through the air
to land smack on his derrière!

Yucky Yummy

Major Payne kept bees to make money
and set up a stall to sell honey.
But pots filled while sneezing,
much coughing and wheezing,
meant it was more yucky than yummy!

"Boy" and Beret

Panic sped across the yard,
her pounding heart on fire.
She had news that could not wait
but crashed into a tyre.

TJ asked her what was up:
she stuttered, "M-Monty's dead.
S-someone coming out the house
is w-wearing him on their head."

Hetty tried to calm her down —
told her she mustn't worry.
Then sent off her brood of chicks
to go and scout for Scurry.

Scurry arrived, but made no sense
of Panic's manic ramble;
told Hetty that her bump on head
had sent her screwball-scramble.

Later, in the barn...

Panic's fears were realised
the minute, if not before,
the "someone" that she said she'd seen
then stepped in through the door.

Winnie spoke: "Looks like a boy,
and the thing plonked on his head
to me looks like a beret."
"Think it's Monty's," Olive said.

The "boy" replied to Winnie
by connecting to her mind.
Conversed with her in silent speak,
but was dumb to his own kind.

Winston asked the boy his name.
He said to call him Gerry.
Then he asked why so much fuss
was made about his beret.

Monty's story was then told
with everyone chipping in.
Said they would launch a mission,
if they knew where to begin.

Gerry said his uncle John
found the beret while out fishing...
Friends dared to hope he'd find a boat
and grant what they were wishing!

Scrub a Tub Tub

Late afternoon, as bubbles filled room
and Major Payne sang in the bath,
Woobot crept in to frown at the din,
but what met his eyes made him laugh.

Loofah in hand, was waved to command
the band to which he sang along.
And to be fair, though notes were all there,
the order he sang them was wrong!

Woofbot snuck away. Had plans that day
to spend some fun time with a mate.
The Major, meanwhile, bathing in style,
scrubbed up to go out on a date!

No Mean Feet

The Major smiled, just couldn't wait
to spend the evening with his date.
It could, indeed, be his last chance
to woo a lady at a dance.

The jazz bash held in Dimple's Square
was to be hosted by the Mayor.
Now, he could boogie to the beat.
But Major Payne had two left feet!

Down on the quay, he met with Pearl
(she had his head in such a whirl),
and when she kissed him on the cheek
he went bright red and couldn't speak!

They'd met by chance, some days before,
while shopping in the Dimple store.
He made a comment on her hat
which led them to a friendly chat.

Paths crossed again, and — most polite —
the Major asked her out that night.
Accepted offer, smiled with glee,
suggesting "jazz bash" on the quay.

The venue, though, was not his choice
(feared music would drown out his voice).
He downed a pint to numb his fear:
his dancing debut now grew near.

Down on the floor, got in the groove,
but when feet tried a nifty move,
Pearl shouted, "STOP! ARRRGH! That'll do!"
Her dainty toes were black and blue!

Apologies came thick and fast,
for fear this date would be their last.
But Pearl, who was so very nice,
said she would soothe her toes with ice.

The Major (who'd had quite a night),
arriving home in bright moonlight,
looked up at twinkling stars above
and told the world: He was in love!

Rat Attack

Gerry came to the barn each day,
to help with chores, have fun and play.
But with the Major out the way,
he'd climb aboard and drive TJ.

TJ's hard lesson in the sea
left him as polite as could be.
Winnie and Winston were his friends
and he'd done much to make amends.

Cheeky chatter on bales of straw
had friends engage in tales galore.
True to say, though, some were wary.
Scurry said his past was scary.

With chirpy cheeps now keen to know
why the mice were numbered so,
asked "007", while Panic slept
to share the secret he had kept...

"While we," said Scurry, "ran around
gobbling up grub on the ground,
we saw a shadow, 'eard a SNAP!
And there we was, stuck in a trap.

The mad old hag of Brimstone Bottom
'ad bad breath, like eggs gone rotten.
She'd thick-rimmed specs, nose like a hook
and wrote down numbers in a book.

Numbers. Numbers. 'Twas no joke!
And all day long 'ere's what she croaked:
'Numbers are and numbers be,
but which one shall I 'ave for tea?'

She branded numbers on our skin,
then got a cage and chucked us in.
We ate no grub, got thin and thinner
so she'd not cook us up for dinner.

We weren't alone. No! Millions more
were caged on shelves or stacked on floor.
In tins she kept dried bugs and fishes
to add more flavour to 'er dishes.

On a shelf where it said: 'BAIT'
were caged-up mice fearing their fate.
At noon each day, it made us quake,
to see 'em fed as snacks to snake.

The old hag didn't 'ave a cat.
She 'ad Hades, a big fat rat.
His heart was black, as was his coat.
'Ad teeth like steel and loved to gloat.

Planned to escape, aware that next
I'd 'ave to smash 'er thick-rimmed specs.
Without 'em, and 'elp from that rat,
she would be blind, much like a bat.

Hades went out. Hag opened cage
and I was ready, full of rage.
I bit 'er hand, then, as it bled,
ran up 'er sleeve and leapt on 'ead.

As she then fell, the plan was done:
she crushed 'er specs with big fat bum.
All those we freed, both big and small,
gave thanks as they shot out the door.

Hades came back. We we took a stand.
But things didn't go quite as we'd planned.
Grabbin' '999', he ripped 'er ear,
which filled 'er eyes with panic and fear.

I waved a stick and poked his eye.
Hades then squealed and said we'd die.
Through field, forest, uphill and down,
till his last breath, he'd hunt us down.

Grabbed Panic's hand and off we shoot,
though 'ad no time to plan a route.
But some miles on, in a wooded glade,
bumped into Baz and his brigade.

The badgers, learning of our plight,
gave us a lift, as day met night.
They really did all that they could
to keep us safe whilst in the wood."

At Panic, Fireside took a peek,
then said that she would like to speak.
They all agreed, and most concise,
she told how she'd made friends with mice:

"I was," she said, "scared as could be,
dumped in a sack tied to a tree.
And then one day, losing all hope
two mice arrived to nibble rope.

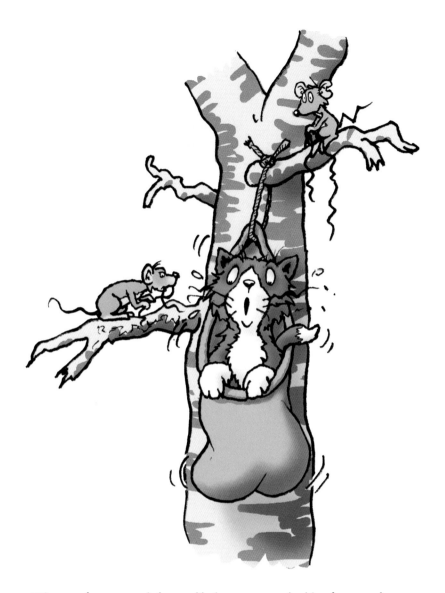

The mice could well have met their end:
I could have killed them there and then.
As you can see, 'twas not their fate
and now they say I'm their best mate."

A voice was heard. It was Marie,
to say that it was time for tea.
Gerry got up, grabbing his coat,
and then announced — "I've found a boat!"

Diamonds and Pearl

The Major frowned in the mirror,
his "chuckle muscle" not funny.
The reason his belly'd ballooned —
loved to eat grub that was scrummy.

Thinking of Pearl he took action
and went for a trial at the gym.
Slogging, though, just to do jogging
soon killed off his will to be slim.

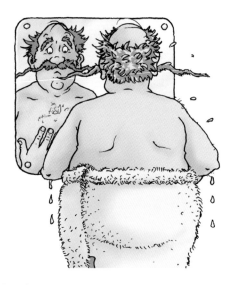

He hoped his Pearl would accept him
(not think his belly too blobby)
and come to love him, warts 'n' all,
even those knees that were knobbly?

One day, whilst in Dimple's Jewellers,
bought a ring, not cheap, but the best!
Later, when he popped the question,
a blushing Pearl smiled to say, "YES!"

Skulduggery

The Major, in his comfy chair,
turned TV on to hear the Mayor
reporting on a robbery
at Dimple's Jewellers on the quay.

In disbelief, moved close to see
the broadcast of CCTV
had Woofbot running in pursuit
of pirates fleeing with their loot.

The Major gulped and spilled his tea
as in came Gerry with Marie.
They caught the tail end of the news,
which left them shocked and most confused.

Woofbot with pirates made no sense.
And Major Payne, now growing tense,
decided he'd drive into town
to see if he could track him down.

Marie went too, but Gerry stayed:
decision that was quickly made,
for fear that Woofbot may be harmed,
would cause his friends to feel alarmed.

Searching the homes for waifs and strays
would take the Major many days,
but he would rather wish and hope
than sit around all day and mope.

With Woofbot gone the mood was grim,
and those who could now searched for him.
Friends needed news to stem their fears
and hoped it would not end in tears.

Moonlight Misson

Monty laid on a rocky floor
where drunken pirates fart and snore,
had friends who knew what they must do
and now had help to see it through.

When Gerry asked who'd like to go,
no prize for guessing who said, "No!"
To force her would have been unkind,
so Panic would be left behind.

The time was nigh, the tides were right,
with moon and stars a welcome sight.
The mission could now go ahead:
by dawn, though, must be back in bed.

Clock was ticking, time to hurry.
List was quickly checked by Scurry.
Then in haste, without a peep,
the motley crew crammed in the jeep.

The horses towed JO3LL to the road
(the one that had those grumpy toads).
Round hooves were sacks to muffle sound
their metal shoes make on the ground.

The Major was out for the night,
so had to get their timing right.
Before the off, checked to confirm
that Olive would signal their return.

The mission's boat was moored downstream
in hopes that it would not be seen.
But as JO3LL then approached with care,
'twas plain to see — it wasn't there!

Boat stuck in reeds, made mood turn black,
till Olive said, "I'll get it back."
She wrapped a rope round hook on bow
and then told Gerry: "Pull it now!"

With time lost getting the boat back
the mission's plans were knocked off track.
With this in mind, on moonlit river,
Gerry felt a nervous shiver.

A course was now set down the Piddle,
through deepest channel in the middle.
Poole Harbour lay at Piddle's mouth,
Old Harry's Rocks had them head south.

A few miles on — disaster struck
which seemed to be the worst of luck!
Boat's engine died in a smoky plume,
filling the crew with gloom and doom.

Then...

A huge wave struck the little boat
and, though the vessel stayed afloat,
as crew were told they must be brave,
Scurry was taken by a wave.

He had quite clearly disappeared
and for his life his friends now feared.
But playful dolphins Flip and Fin
now set their sights on saving him.

What they did next soon rid despair,
for Scurry, launched into the air,
was grabbed in flight ('twas quite a show).
The dolphins then gave them a tow.

Paye Island loomed and, once ashore,
Gerry then made the boat secure.
With all the crew now safely out,
Scurry and Sneak flew off to scout.

In no time, found the pirate's lair
and counted three still hiding there.
Monty, whom they had come to save,
was thought to be inside the cave.

Found Woofbot tied up to a tree
and snipped the rope to set him free.
They then made off, no time to lose
as pirates sat round slurping booze.

With Woofbot safe, all hearts were healed:
excitement, though, swiftly concealed.
The stakes were high, all knew their part
and fully briefed, 'twas time to start.

Out of harm's way, the groups were formed
before the pirate's cave was stormed.
On count of three, all hell broke loose
and pirate crooks hurled much abuse...

Shimmy struck fear into their hearts.
Napoleon ripped their pants apart.
Scurry bashed drum — BOOM! BANG! BANG!
With mayhem spread by rest of gang.

As chaos reigned — confusion spread.
One pirate fell and bashed his head.
Gerry, meanwhile, sneaked by the fire
to grab Monty and his attire.

All done — he sounded the retreat
and creatures now, by wing and feet,
fled to the beach, increasing pace,
aware two pirates now gave chase.

Gerry then issued Sneak his cue
(he'd been well primed with what to do).
Once he and Olive returned with net
the trap was well and truly set.

The boat was tethered to the jetty.
Keeping watch was frantic Hetty.
But once the fishing net was dropped
the pirates, in their tracks, were stopped!

Then, as the darkness crumbled away,
Shimmy announced he planned to stay.
He'd found a mate of his own kind,
so thought it best to stay behind.

Shimmy's friends, whose trust he'd won,
thanked him for all that he had done.
Then Flip and Fin towed boat to sea.
Crew homeward bound to JO3LL, on quay...

In Monty's jacket, back at home,
Gerry then found a pirate's phone.
Soon came to mind what to do next,
so to police, he sent a text!

Taken

Jeep back in barn, the horses too,
the crew had done all they could do.
With Monty, though, in such a state,
had rescue mission come too late?

As weary souls slept in the straw,
Scurry responded to a call.
A worried TJ'd come to say:
"Panic's been taken far away.

The thing what grabbed her was a rat.
A scary black beast, big and fat..."
(Scurry had thought her safe with hens,
with whom she had made many friends.)

A new day dawned, and full of fear,
Scurry woke Olive, who made it clear
that they must now take to the sky.
No time to tell the others why.

To Brimstone Bottom, off they flew
with field and forest in full view.
A mercy mission for a friend
whom Scurry'd vowed he would defend.

Tracking west (no time to dither),
spied their quarry near a river.
Scurry, down on the bridge at last,
then told Hades, "You shall not pass!"

Hades hurled Panic to her doom
(which raised the stakes) but none too soon,
as mouse and rat squared up to fight,
Olive caught Panic in full flight.

Out of harm's way, she set her free.
Then from a branch held breath to see
that in a rage, on yonder ridge,
Scurry hurled Hades off the bridge.

Once Panic had said she was all right,
they took off on a homeward flight.
Back in the barn and safe with friends
told all how Hades met his end.

The Day After the Night Before

Pirate arrest made headline news.
Chief Constable airing his views
on lessons "pirates" would be taught,
though knew not how the crooks were caught.

For Major Payne the great surprise
(which had him mopping teary eyes),
came when he opened up his door
and Woofbot offered him a paw.

Oh joy of joy, so full of glee.
Marie came in and made the tea.
Woofbot received some doggy treats
whilst lying at his master's feet.

But in the barn, all hearts were down:
Monty lay lifeless on the ground.
They placed the beret on his head
and in the hush, no words were said.

Hoping a storm would see him healed,
they staked him out, back in the field.
And, though friends feared he'd met his doom,
they kept the faith he'd be back soon.

Bother and Bliss

"COCKADOODLEDOO!"

As Major Payne sprang out of bed,
(on this the day that he'd be wed)
he had no time to curse that cock
whilst searching for a matching sock.

Wide awake and busy fussing
(made a change from all that cussing),
he ran a bath in which to wallow —
quite unaware of what would follow.

Plans were afoot and all on track.
The Major'd scrubbed and polished tack.
Promised Pearl a horse-drawn carriage
would convey her to their marriage.

The clock was ticking — weather fine.
Jeep sped him to the church on time.
'Twould be the best day of his life,
once he and Pearl were man and wife.

The organ started, made him smile:
his Pearl was walking down the aisle.
He dared to peek — ARRRGH! No! By golly!
She was arm-in-arm with Wally!

As his blood boiled and eyes went wide,
he wished for a hole in which to hide.
Oh, what a nightmare! Must wake up.
He pinched himself, but no such luck.

When Wally whispered, "Pearl's my twin,"
the Major turned to scowl at him.
He'd set a trap. This was no joke.
He really was a rotten bloke!

The congregation rose to sing.
Arthur confirmed he'd got the ring.
When guests were told that they may sit,
poor Major Payne felt such a twit.

This was a sham, he'd been deceived
and thought it time to take his leave.
But Pearl then smiled and caught his hand,
so things moved on, just as she'd planned.

As vows were spoken, wet with sweat,
the Major had but one regret:
to that "wally" whom he'd hated
he'd now forever be related!

Once Major Payne had kissed his bride
and mingled with the guests outside,
his mood was swiftly lightened up
when at his foot was Woofbot's pup.

The woofadoodles were so cute.
Their playful antics were a hoot.
They had the guests laughing out loud,
which made Posh-Paws and Woofbot proud.

But things soon got quite out of hand:
the photo session not as planned.
But long before the chaos spread,
the puppies went off home to bed.

Winston and Winnie, standing by,
saw that the bridesmaid caught their eye.
But when she waved, oh, what a shock —
it was young Gerry in a frock!

She told her friends in silent speak
the secret that she chose to keep.
They then agreed, 'twas quite a ploy
convincing them she was a boy.

Geraldine, fostered by Marie,
was now as happy as could be.
She'd found a world, complete and shared
with loyal friends for whom she cared.

Major Payne had married a Coop
and, though at first not cock-a-hoop,
his Wally woes were soon forgotten
with wedded bliss in Happy Bottom!

Shocking...

While Monty's friends all feared the worst
(that by those "pirates" he'd been cursed),
a lightning storm ripped sky apart,
sending a charge to shock his heart...